Phonics Friends

# Umberto's Summer Day
## The Sound of Short U

The Child's World

*By Cecilia Minden and Joanne Meier*

**The Child's World**

Published in the United States of America
by The Child's World®
PO Box 326
Chanhassen, MN 55317-0326
800-599-READ
www.childsworld.com

A special thank you to the Hopkins family for allowing
Coconut to be photographed in mud!

The Child's World®: Mary Berendes, Publishing Director

Editorial Directions, Inc.: E. Russell Primm, Editorial Director
and Project Editor; Katie Marsico, Associate Editor; Judith
Shiffer, Associate Editor and School Media Specialist;
Linda S. Koutris, Photo Researcher and Selector

The Design Lab: Kathleen Petelinsek, Design and Page
Production

Photographs ©: Corbis/Carl and Ann Purcell: 10; Corbis/
David Stoecklein: 12; Corbis/Ronnie Kaufman: cover, 4;
Corbis/Steve Prezant: 20; Corbis/Tria Giovan: 8; Flanagan
Publishing Services: 16; Getty Images/Photodisc Red/
Geostock: 6; Getty Images/Photodisc Green/Ryan McVay:
14; E. Russell Primm: 18.

**Library of Congress Cataloging-in-Publication Data**
Minden, Cecilia.
  Umberto's summer day : the sound of short U / by
Cecilia Minden and Joanne Meier.
    p. cm. — (Phonics friends)
  Summary: Simple text featuring the sound of the short "u"
describes some of the ways a boy enjoys a summer day.
  ISBN 1-59296-316-1 (library bound : alk. paper) [1.
English language—Phonetics. 2. Reading.] I. Meier, Joanne
D. II. Title. III. Series.
  PZ7.M6539Uk 2004
  [E]—dc22                                    2004003541

**Note to parents and educators:**

*The Child's World® has created Phonics Friends with the goal of exposing children to engaging stories and pictures that assist in phonics development. The books in the series will help children learn the relationships between the letters of written language and the individual sounds of spoken language. This contact helps children learn to use these relationships to read and write words.*

*The books in this series follow a similar format. An introductory page, to be read by an adult, introduces the child to the phonics feature, or sound, that will be highlighted in the book. Read this page to the child, stressing the phonic feature. Help the student learn how to form the sound with her mouth. The Phonics Friends story and engaging photographs follow the introduction. At the end of the story, word lists categorize the feature words into their phonic element. Additional information on using these lists is on The Child's World® Web site listed at the top of this page.*

*Each book in this series has been carefully written to meet specific readability requirements. Close attention has been paid to elements such as word count, sentence length, and vocabulary. Readability formulas measure the ease with which the text can be read and understood. Each Phonics Friends book has been analyzed using the Spache readability formula. For more information on this formula, as well as the levels for each of the books in this series please visit The Child's World® Web site.*

*Reading research suggests that systematic phonics instruction can greatly improve students' word recognition, spelling, and comprehension skills. The Phonics Friends series assists in the teaching of phonics by providing students with important opportunities to apply their knowledge of phonics as they read words, sentences, and text.*

The letter *u* makes two sounds.

The long sound of *u* sounds like *u* as in:

cute and *tube*.

The short sound of *u* sounds like *u* as in:

*mud* and *up*.

In this book, you will read words that have the short *u* sound as in:

*bugs, ducks, run,* and *mud*.

Umberto is happy.

It is a bright summer day.

There is so much to do!

Umberto likes to hunt for bugs.
Some bugs are as small as
buttons. Some bugs hum
when they fly.

Umberto finds ducks. He
feeds the ducks from a cup.

A duck jumps to get the food.

He must be very hungry!

Umberto likes to run.

His puppy, Tuffy, runs too.

Tuffy runs in the mud.

Now his fur is full of mud.

"Oh, Tuffy, you look funny!" says Umberto. "I'll get the mud off you."

Umberto brushes Tuffy.

He rubs off the mud.

It is time for supper.

We're having bread

and butter. Yummy!

# Fun Facts

Did you know that people have recorded eating 462 different types of bugs? Someone even came up with a recipe for chocolate chirpie cookies—a special treat that contains chocolate chips, chopped nuts, and crickets! But be sure and talk to your parents before you get hungry and head for your backyard. Not all bugs are safe to eat, and even the ones that are usually need to be prepared a certain way.

Do you like the warm weather in summer? When the weather is chilly in winter, remember that people who live south of the equator are enjoying their summer. The equator is an imaginary line that runs around the middle of the earth at a halfway point between the North and South poles. During our winter months, the earth turns in a way that makes the sun closer to people who live south of the equator.

# Activity

### Keeping a Bug House

Visit your local library to learn about keeping a bug house. You can either buy a ready-made bug house or use household items such as old jam or pickle jars with holes punched in the lids. Check to make sure that the bugs you plan to keep will get along with each other. Find out what each bug will need to eat. Consider releasing the bugs back into the wild after you have studied them for a few days.

# To Learn More

### Books
### About the Sound of Short U
Ballard, Peg, and Cynthia Klingel. *Fun! The Sound of Short U*. Chanhassen, Minn.:
The Child's World, 2000.

### About Bugs
Carter, David A. *Alpha Bugs: A Pop-Up Alphabet*. New York: Little Simon, 1994.
Shields, Carol Diggory, and Scott Nash (illustrator). *The Bugliest Bug*. Cambridge,
Mass.: Candlewick Press, 2002.

### About Mud
Quinn, Lin, and Ronnie Rooney (illustrator). *The Best Mud Pie*. New York:
Children's Press, 2001.
Ryan, Pam Muñoz, and David McPhail (illustrator). *Mud Is Cake*. New York:
Hyperion Books for Children, 2002.

### About Summer
Dotlich, Rebecca Kai, and Jan Spivey Gilchrist (illustrator). *Lemonade Sun and
Other Summer Poems*. Honesdale, Pa.: Wordsong/Boyds Mills Press, 1998.
Hurwitz, Johanna, and Heather Maione (illustrator). *Summer with Elisa*. New
York: Morrow Junior Books, 2000.

### Web Sites
### Visit our home page for lots of links about the Sound of Short U:
*http://www.childsworld.com/links.html*

Note to Parents, Teachers, and Librarians: We routinely check our Web links to make sure
they're safe, active sites—so encourage your readers to check them out!

# Short U
# Feature Words

## Proper Names

Tuffy                    Umberto

## Feature Words in Medial Position

bug                      jump
butter                   much
button                   mud
cup                      must
duck                     puppy
full                     rub
funny                    run
hum                      summer
hungry                   supper
hunt                     yummy

## Feature Word with Blends

brush

# About the Authors

*Cecilia Minden, PhD, directs the Language and Literacy Program at the Harvard Graduate School of Education. She is a reading specialist with classroom and administrative experience in grades K–12. She earned her PhD in reading education from the University of Virginia. Cecilia and her husband Dave Cupp enjoy sharing their love of reading with their granddaughter Chelsea.*

*Joanne Meier, PhD, has worked as an elementary school teacher and university professor. She earned her BA in early childhood education from the University of South Carolina, and her MEd and PhD in education from the University of Virginia. She currently works as a literacy consultant for schools and private organizations. Joanne Meier lives with her husband Eric, and spends most of her time chasing her two daughters, Kella and Erin, and her two cats, Sam and Gilly, in Charlottesville, Virginia.*